For Gemma

12.89

89B2436

The Trouble With Elephants
Copyright © 1988 by Chris Riddell
First published in Great Britain by Walker Books Ltd, London
Printed in Hong Kong by South China Printing Company
All rights reserved.
1 2 3 4 5 6 7 8 9 10
First American Edition

Library of Congress Cataloging-in-Publication Data
Riddell, Chris.
    The trouble with elephants / written and illustrated by
Chris Riddell. — 1st American ed.
        p.   cm.
    Summary: A little girl describes the various problems
with elephants, but decides the real trouble with elephants
is that you can't help but love them.
    ISBN 0-397-32272-0 : $
    ISBN 0-397-32273-9 (lib. bdg.): $
    [1. Elephants—Fiction.]   I. Title.
PZ7.R41618Tr 1988   87-24963
[E]—dc19   CIP
                                                                  AC

The Trouble With Elephants

Written and illustrated by

Chris Riddell

J. B. Lippincott   New York

The trouble with elephants is . . .

they spill the bathwater
when they get in . . .

and they leave a pink elephant
ring when they get out.

They take all the sheets, and
they snore elephant snores, which
rattle the windowpanes.

The only way to wake a sleeping
elephant is to shout "Mouse!"
in its ear.

Then it will slide down the
banister to breakfast.

Elephants travel four in a car—two
in the front and two in the back.

You can always tell when an elephant is visiting because there'll be a car outside with three elephants in it.

Sometimes elephants ride bicycles . . .

but not very often.

The trouble with elephants is that on elephant picnics they eat all the cupcakes before you've finished your first one.

Elephants drink their lemonade through their trunks, and if you're not looking, they drink yours too.

On elephant picnics they play games like leap-elephant and jump rope, which they're good at.

And sometimes they play hide-and-seek,
which they're not very good at.

The trouble with elephants is . . .

well, there are all sorts of troubles . . .

all sorts of troubles . . .

but the real trouble is . . .

you can't help but love them.